OTHER BOOKS BY JUSTIN JOHNSON

Gertrude the Chubby Unicorn: Gertrude Takes the Cake

Gertrude the Chubby Unicorn: Gertrude Eats A Dog

Gertrude the Chubby Unicorn: Gertrude's Donut Shot Delight

Gertrude the Chubby Unicorn: Gertrude Grills It Up

Zack and Zebo: The Complete Series

The Jungle: The Complete Series

Coby Collins: The Complete Series

Grade School Super Hero: The Complete Trilogy

The Goldilocks Theorem

Farty Marty and Other Stories

Do Not Feed the Zombies and Other Stories

The Disgusting and Heartwarming Collection

Trip of a Lifetime

The Christmas Mix Up

The Night Nothing Went Right

The Great Tree Lighting

The Card

Scab and Beads: The Complete Series

THE CHRISTMAS MIX UP

JUSTIN JOHNSON

CCS
Publishing

CONTENTS

INTRODUCTION

Hello and Welcome to the Christmas Season.

This book is very special to me...perhaps, the most special story I've written to date.

You see, my oldest daughter and I were reading stories one night before bed, as is customary in the Johnson household. When we finished reading our stories for the night, she looked at me and said, "Why don't you write a story about Santa?"

I told her that I already had. That story's called "The Trip of a Lifetime." I even reminded her that I'd read it to her already.

She nodded and let me know that she liked it, but it wasn't her favorite. Which is funny, because that was not the reaction I received the first time I read it to her.

But for some reason, in November of 2017, she

decided that she needed me to write more Santa stories. Which isn't hard for me. I love sitting at my desk, listening to Christmas music and just imagining how amazing the North Pole must be.

I started this story last year, and then got side tracked. So, I put it up for a while. And forgot about it.

Then this year rolled around. Over this past summer, I published some stories about a chubby unicorn named Gertrude that my daughters both really enjoyed. I've got a few more of those in the tank. They want me to write twenty of them…but it'll be close to eight, I think.

Anyway, my oldest came up with another story idea, which, as of the writing of this introduction is already underway. It got me thinking about last year and the story I didn't finish.

So, this is it! This is the book that I started with my daughter last year. She wrote her version and I wrote mine.

I think it's pretty okay. And because of the conversations my daughter and I have shared about it over the last year, it will always be among my favorite books that I've written.

I hope you enjoy The Christmas Mix Up.

Merry Christmas,

Justin Johnson

October 21, 2018

PROLOGUE

I stood there in the middle of Lincoln Street, the snow coming down in big fluffy flakes. I had just grabbed the letter from the mailbox and was getting ready to head up the front steps to my house, when I noticed my name on the front of the envelope.

Ms. Penelope Ann Dingman.

And the return address.

I could barely move when I noticed that this letter was sent from the North Pole.

The snow flakes were falling on it and the ink that had been used to write the addresses was starting to run as wet spots emerged on the envelope.

"Nelly," my mother called, throwing open the front door. "Come inside, child. You're going to catch a cold."

I held up the envelope in my hand, unable to speak. I

just stood there in the middle of the sidewalk, looking dumb.

"Move your right foot forward," my mother said, smiling. "And then after that, your left. You can do it, dear. Come on." And then she turned and walked down the hallway laughing and leaving the door open.

I eventually found my footing and walked myself up the steps and into the house.

I kicked my boots off, dropped my backpack and hung my jacket up before rushing upstairs to my bedroom and slamming the door behind me.

It was a little louder than I'd wanted it to be, but my mother was so busy cooking dinner that she didn't even mention it.

I sprawled out on my stomach across my bed and ran my hand along the top edge of the envelope before sticking my finger under the loose flap and ripping it open. My finger carved a jagged ditch through the wet, white crease.

When I popped it open, I was surprised to see how tiny the sheet of paper it had carried was. It was only about half the length of the envelope they'd put it in. It was folded into three, with two sharp creases running the width of it, placed about two neat inches apart from one another.

I closed my eyes and brought the letter to my nose, expecting to smell something special. I was thinking maybe candy canes or cinnamon, perhaps some orange peel or pine. But I smelled none of those things. What I smelled was oily and earthy, like the smell of a furnace burning.

I opened my eyes and took a closer look at the letter. It was covered with black smudges of soot.

Finally, I decided to read it.

And that's the moment I realized that a huge mistake had occurred. And if I didn't find a way to fix this mix up fast, my Christmas was going to be the pits.

1

"Can you believe this!" I exclaimed as I held the letter up to my best friend, Lindsay.

Lindsay Bellamore Cooper, that's how she introduced herself to people, stared in disbelief as she started to read out loud.

I yanked the letter away. "Not here!" I shouted, as I moved my eyes around the hallway. There were a lot of kids putting their coats and boots in their lockers before the morning bell rang, and if any of them caught the gist of this letter, my reputation was caput.

"Okay," she said, her feelings clearly hurt. "But just remember, you're the one that stuck it in my face." She picked her books up off the floor and stormed into our classroom, leaving me alone in the hallway with everyone else.

I tucked the letter back in my folder as quickly as I could and proceeded toward the room myself, not wanting to appear frazzled.

I took my seat next to her and whispered, "I'm sorry."

"Apology accepted," she said, putting her nose in the air.

"I'd still appreciate your help, though," I said, leaning in close. "You see, I have no idea how to fix this. And it's kind of time sensitive."

"How much time are we talking about?"

"Before Christmas for sure. But sooner would be better," I answered.

Lindsay took a look at her agenda calendar and noted that we had one week before Christmas.

"Seven days," she said, meeting my eyes with hers. I could see the doubt in them.

But it didn't stop me from saying, "Or less."

She sighed and said, "Come to my house after school. We'll take a closer look at that letter and figure something out."

"Thanks," I said.

Then our teacher walked up to the board and started the lessons, and the letter was put away for the day.

2

*L*indsay Bellamore Cooper lived with her mother, their two cats, Hans and Frans, and her pesky four year old brother, Jeffry in Elm Crest Apartments, about two block from my house.

Her mother never cooked like my mother. Instead she ordered their dinner every night over the telephone. Tonight she'd ordered pizza. I salivated as I walked in the door and the smell hit my nose. I could pick up hints of sausage and green peppers in the air.

Lindsay walked straight through the kitchen and down the hallway toward the back of the apartment where her bedroom was located.

I stopped dead in my tracks.

"I love pizza," I proclaimed.

Lindsay turned and shrugged her shoulders and said,

"eh," and then turned back toward her room and began shedding her coat.

Taking one final sniff, I put my head down and followed her.

Now, it should be noted that Lindsay, though she is smart as a whip, and capable of solving some of the world's most difficult problems, is a complete slob.

Her bed was covered with papers and clothes and lip balm containers. Crayons and pencils were strewn about on the floor, and she had a nice collection of purses and backpacks, with broken straps or ripped out zippers, in each corner.

She had a TV on her dresser. Each drawer was opened to varying degrees, and disorganized patterns of clothing and color were popping out and hanging over the edge of each one of them. Around the TV she had various pieces of jewelry, which looked like something that might be found on the Island of Misfit Toys. There were also pictures of her favorite places and a framed image of her with her favorite singer. They'd met after a concert her mother had taken her to last year. Both of them were holding each other close and looking out at me as I studied it.

"Best night ever!" she shouted as she jumped on her bed.

"Pardon me?" I asked.

Lindsay pointed at the picture on her dresser. "That

was the best night of my life," she exclaimed. And then she rolled back and started kicking her feet wildly in the air. "And the best night I'll ever have. OMG, she was so good. And all the costume changes were mesmerizing. She's what every pop star wants to be!"

"I see," I said, moving away from the picture and looking for a place to sit and put my stuff down. I couldn't find one. There was junk everywhere.

"Just throw your things on the floor and hop up here," Lindsay said. She patted a spot on her bed and pushed the papers that were occupying the spot onto the floor, revealing a floral patterned comforter. "And don't forget the letter," she said. "I still don't know what this whole thing is about." She reached over and turned on the light that was on her nightstand.

I put my backpack on the floor and pulled the letter from the front pocket before planting myself on top of a soft, purple rose.

Lindsay held out her hand and said, "Alright, let me have a look at what we're dealing with."

I handed over the letter and watched her unfold it.

"It smells awful," she gasped. "And what's with all these black smudges? What'd you do to this thing, Nelly?"

"I didn't do anything," I said, defensively. "That's how it came."

She looked at me with the same eyes and furrowed brow I would have expected to get from my mother.

"That's the truth!" I exclaimed.

"Let me see the envelope," she said.

I handed it over to her and watched as she examined the outside of it, and then the inside of it. She turned it over in her hands and looked at the writing on the front.

"Then North Pole, eh?" she said. "Do you know anyone who's trying to get even with you? Trick you somehow?"

"No," I said. "Why?"

"Nothing," she replied. "It's just...I've never seen a letter from the North Pole before and it seems odd that they would have time to send them out to kids this time of year. I mean, from everything I've read and heard, the elves and Santa are just getting into full swing, right?"

I nodded my head. "That's what I was thinking, too. I was shocked when I pulled that out of my mailbox. And then I opened it and I was even more surprised."

She tossed the envelope back onto her bed. It landed on some papers that were piled haphazardly at the end of it. I instinctively reached for it and held it tenderly in my hands. Regardless of what the letter said, I had received something that most kids would never get. I was going to cherish the parts of it that I could.

Lindsay unfolded the letter and read aloud:

Dear Penelope A. Dingman,

We regret to inform you that you have been put on the Naughty List this year.

Your behavior has been far from acceptable and for Santa and the elves to make and deliver presents to you this year would be contradictory to his message of moral excellence.

It is with heavy hearts that we are notifying you of the coal that will be delivered to your stocking this year.

Please do better next year.

Sincerely,
Santa Claus and Company

"This is not good," she said. "Not good at all."

3

I could feel the sweat forming on the palms of my hands. My forehead was also getting cold and wet.

It had been one thing to read the letter to myself, in the privacy of my own bedroom. But then, I knew that it was just me and the folks at the North Pole who knew about the promised coal and my bad behavior.

But now it was all out in the open. Lindsay knew about it. And even though she had been my best friend ever since that first day of kindergarten when we sat on the bus together, a pit of dread formed in my belly. Could I really trust her to keep this to herself? I mean, we weren't exactly talking about the kind of secret one normally tells their best friend. We weren't talking about a small crush on a boy, or sneaking an extra piece of candy from the treat jar.

We were talking about something much, much bigger. And I had a reputation as a good girl at school. My parents, of course, knew that I could be a handful. But everyone else thought of me as 'that nice girl, Nelly'. And, I guess, if I was being completely honest with myself, I had started to think of myself in those terms too. And that's why this letter came as such a shock.

Even telling Lindsay about it might have been a step too far. But letting her read it, on her bed, while I watched every single twitch and facial contortion she made, felt like something that I might come to regret.

There was nothing I could do about it now. It was out. The only thing that I could think of that would take this back would be telling her that I made the whole thing up and that I had sent myself a fake letter as a prank. And then we could laugh the whole thing off and she would call me an idiot and I would agree. She'd probably tell everyone at school about the silly thing I'd done and we would all laugh about how stupid the whole thing had been. And then, when we came back from Christmas vacation, they'd all be talking about the cool things they'd gotten in their stockings and under the tree and I'd have to say things like, "me too!" or, "wow, that's great!," never really able to tell them what I'd gotten, because the whole letter thing hadn't actually been a lie.

It had been real. And this year, I wasn't getting anything for Christmas, except a lesson on behavior.

"We have to do something about this," I heard Lindsay say as she flipped the letter over in her hand and checked the back of it. There was nothing written on it, of course. But Lindsay was thorough. That's why I was going to her for help in the first place.

"This letter can't possibly be about you." She handed the paper back to me. "I mean, you're one of the best behaved kids in the school for crying out loud. How many times have you won the Principal's Award?"

"I don't know," I lied. "Six or eight times, maybe." I knew it was actually nine, but I was trying to be modest.

"Exactly," Lindsay said. "Something wonky's going on here. And we need to find out what it is and stop it before your Christmas is completely ruined!"

4

*S*he hopped off her bed in one quick jump and said, "Follow me!"

I did as I was told and we ended up in the corner of the living room. Her mother had just gotten home and was sitting on the couch watching TV.

"Hey, mom," Lindsay said. "How was your day?"

"Exhausting," her mother replied, flipping through the channels absentmindedly. "I just need a few minutes to relax before I do anything else."

"Got it," Lindsay said. "We'll just be over here."

I followed her to a computer in the corner of the living room.

"If you girls are going to play any games, can you just keep the volume down so I can hear my shows?" her mother asked politely.

"Sure thing, mom." Lindsay gave her mother a thumbs up and pressed the button to turn the computer on.

Within a matter of moments, we were staring at a bright blue screen. Lindsay typed in some letters and numbers, but they were too fast for me to see.

Then there was a screen with folders and some other pictures that I wasn't familiar with.

Already, I was relieved because my friend Lindsay was showing me things I didn't know about. There was no way I could have ever done this on my own. I felt kind of helpless as I watched her click on things and open the imaginary folders on the screen. I thought that I should be able to do these things on my own.

But I was also grateful that I had someone like her in my life to help me in situations like this.

"Here's something," she said, sitting up straight and leaning in toward the illuminated screen. She brought her finger up to point. "Do you see that, there!"

I leaned in and looked at the tip of her finger. It was pointing to a train schedule.

"I think I see what you're pointing at, but I'm not sure I understand why you're pointing at it."

"This is the schedule for all of the trains that are going to the North Pole. There aren't many of them, but there are a few. And the good news is, they seem to be leaving before Christmas."

"That is good!" I shouted. I covered my mouth and gave a quick glance to her mother, who was looking at me with a smirk on her face.

"It's okay, honey," she said, "just try to keep it down and contain the excitement if you can."

"Okay," I nodded. "I will, I promise."

And then I put my hand over my mouth and gave Lindsay a high-five.

"There's just one problem," she noted.

"What's that?"

"These tickets are thirty dollars a piece."

"Oh, that's not a problem," I gloated. "My grandparents gave me a lot of money for my birthday this past year. I still have about eighty dollars left. That should more than cover the cost for both of us."

"Both of us?" She asked. I could hear the surprise in her voice. "I'm not going."

"What do you mean you're not going?" I asked. "You have to go. There's no way I could make it without you. Please!" I begged.

She looked over at her mother. "Mom, can I go to the North Pole with Penelope tomorrow after school?"

"Not a chance," her mother answered dryly.

Lindsay turned back to look at me. "See," she said. "I can't go."

"But I need you," I protested. "I absolutely, one

hundred percent, need you to come along with me on this one."

"Sorry." She shrugged her shoulders. "You heard the lady. And, don't take this the wrong way...but, *I'm* not the one on the 'Naughty List'."

It took me a minute to accept the truth that was playing out before me. But if I was going to salvage anything from this Christmas, I was going to have to suck it up and deal with the hand I'd been dealt.

"I understand," I said. "Would you, at least, be able to help me order my ticket."

"Sure," she said.

A few clicks later, and a couple of reassurances that I would give her the thirty dollars when I got back, and I had the ticket in my hand.

I put it in my backpack and thanked Lindsay on my way out the door.

"Don't mention it," she said.

I knew I'd see her the next day in school, but I thought I might have kind of a lot on my mind. After all, I was preparing to go to the home of one Chris Kringle.

5

*T*he day was like a whirlwind.

And then there I was, at the train station. There were people bustling around to and fro, lugging suitcases and dragging wheeled luggage behind them. Most of the people were older — grown ups who looked like they'd never find happiness again. I stood there for a moment, looking around the station, wondering how many of them might've also gotten letters themselves about being on Santa's naughty list.

I know it made me miserable for a while. But I was moving on. I wasn't going let this little thing get me down. Of course, I didn't really belong on the naughty list in the first place, right? I mean, it must've been an accident.

Maybe these grumpy grumps really did belong on the list.

Perhaps they'd already talked to the big man, himself, and he'd told them matter of factly that they were on the right list and unless they shaped up and started acting the right way they would have no hopes of ever coming off of it.

If that was the case, then I completely understood their sour pusses and grouchy demeanors.

Before I'd left for school for the day, I'd left my mother and father a note on the table, explaining everything in great detail.

As I navigated through my school day, I couldn't help but look over my shoulder, half expecting to see my parents in the hallway beckoning me to come with them so that they could take me home and tie me up and make it impossible for me to get on the train to the North Pole. But I'd made it through the day and they hadn't shown up so far as I could tell.

And now that I was here in line, waiting to board the train, that same feeling came over me. I was sure that at some point before this adventure could even get off the ground, my parents would come in and swoop me up. And that would be horrible. If that happened, I'd never get off the naughty list. Never.

"The next train to the North Pole will begin boarding now," a voice boomed through the speaker of the station.

I took one last glance around, shrugged my shoulders, picked up my bag and headed for the train, ticket in hand. I walked with my head down, almost sulking. Believe it or not, I was actually a little saddened that my parents hadn't shown up. It felt almost like they didn't care.

The line to board the train moved fairly quickly, and I was in front of a portly little man in a matter of moments. He was wearing a navy blue suit and had a curly mustache on his face that made me smile.

"Ticket please," he said, reaching out his hand.

I gave him my ticket and he eyed it suspiciously.

"Are you alone?" he asked.

"Yes, sir," I answered. It felt weird to call him sir. I knew he was older than I, but he wasn't much taller than the tallest fourth grader at my school.

He looked at me, his gaze penetrating my eyes and making me feel much smaller. And then he whipped his head around and began surveying the platform where others were boarding. It was almost as if he was looking for my parents to come running and claim ownership of me.

He took out a scanner and pointed a red laser at my ticket. I heard a beep and then he handed my ticket back to me.

"Enjoy your trip to the North Pole little girl," he said cheerfully enough.

"Thank you," I said.

I took the ticket and tucked it in the front of my back-pack, then I moved to my seat. I was surprised at how empty the car was. There weren't many people at all. Maybe ten or so. And I was the only kid.

There was a seat in the back, near a window that was overlooking the platform. I moved to it and sat down, thinking that it would be nice to watch the people as they boarded the train.

That's when I saw the sight that made my heart stop. It simultaneously filled me with hope and cheer and dread and fear.

My mother was talking to the man I'd just spoken to. My father was right behind her. They were speaking loudly, and both of their faces were extremely animated as they described me. They brought their hands up and down in big, dramatic gestures.

And then finally, I heard the man tell them, "I'll hold your tickets here. Why don't you go in and have a look and see if you can find her."

6

I had to hide. There was nothing else to it. If my parents saw me here before the train left the station, they'd take me home with them and I'd never get to speak to Santa about the terrible mix up that had occurred.

I heard my mother first.

"Penelope?" she called out. "Nelly honey, if you're on this train, please just come out."

My father was next. "Yeah, Nel. You're not going to be in trouble if you just come to us now."

The man who'd taken my ticket walked into the train and told my parents, "She can't have gotten too far. She just handed me her ticket and boarded this car less than five minutes before you folks came looking for her."

I was crouched in the last row behind the seats.

My eyes were closed and I had my hands together and I was praying for this one thing to just go my way.

It didn't take long for their footsteps to reach the back of the train.

"I don't get it," I heard my mother say. "The man said she'd come in just a few moments before us. You don't think she went to another car do you?"

It was a few seconds before my father answered.

"I don't think so," he said, his deep voice was pensive and low, like he was thinking about something.

In that short moment, I knew exactly what he was thinking about, and it spelled trouble for me.

"I played hide and seek with Penelope enough times when she was younger to know that she likes to bank on the fact that you're not going to find her," I heard him tell my mother.

"So, what does that mean?" she asked. There was a lot of worry and irritation in her voice.

"She was fond of tucking herself into small corners on the floor. I always advised her against it. Time and time again, but she kept doing it. She's stubborn like that. I told her a million times that if you just sit there and someone does eventually find you…"

His voice trailed off and fell silent.

And when I brought my head up from my hands, he was standing right there in the aisle looking down at me.

"You have nowhere to go," I finished his sentence.

7

"*S*tand up," my father said.

I shook my head. If I was going to get off of this train, my parents were going to have to drag me off in front of all of these people.

And knowing my parents the way I do, that wasn't going to happen.

So I just sat there.

It was my only hope.

"Come on, honey," my mother said. "We're not mad at you. I promise. We're a little confused and you've certainly got some explaining to do, but we're not mad."

"I'm not leaving this train," I said into my crossed arms. "If you want to go home, you're going home without me. I have to get to the North Pole. It's urgent and nobody's going to stop me."

"Alright," my father said. He sat down in the seat next to the one I was hiding under. "Tell me this: Why is it so important for you to go to the North Pole?"

It was an innocent enough question. His voice was calm and I knew he wasn't totally mad at me. He just wanted to know the real reason.

I burst into tears. I cried harder than I think I'd ever cried in my life. Then I grabbed my bag and brought it up to my chest and unzipped the front pocket. I pulled the letter out and handed it up to him, keeping my eyes on the floor.

I could hear my mother move herself into position so she could see it with him.

"Oh, dear," she said a few seconds later.

"Oh, dear is right," my father agreed. "I'm going to ask you another question."

I nodded and looked up at him and my mother.

"We see you at home, and we think you're pretty good. Are you doing things that we don't know about that would make this letter necessary?"

I shook my head.

"Are you certain?" my mother asked. "Can you think of anything that you're doing at school, anybody you may have been unkind to?"

"No," I managed.

"So you think this is one big mix up?" my father asked.

I nodded.

"And that's why you're on the train to the North Pole?"

"Yes."

"And you somehow think that you're going to convince Santa to put you back on the Nice List?"

"Uh-huh."

He took a look at my mother. I could see their eyes meet and then they both nodded at each other.

My father turned back to me and said, "Well you'd better get into that seat and buckle up. It looks like we're going on a family adventure."

"Really?" I asked. I was shocked. Never in a million years did I expect my parents to be okay with me going on this trip, let alone want to go with me.

"Yeah," my father said. "Your mother and I have never been to the North Pole, and we've certainly never met Santa. This will be a real treat for us too...if things work out, of course, and he's not too busy."

I made my way to my feet and straightened up my clothes before sitting in the seat and buckling my seat belt.

My father buckled his seat belt too.

My mother moved to the row of seats in front of us and put her purse in the seat next to the window.

"Before I sit down, I just have one question."

"What's that?" I asked.

She held up a ten dollar bill and said, "Who wants hot chocolate?"

8

*T*he train ride was really long. Nothing at all like I thought it would be. I don't know where I got the notion that there would be men in fancy suits dancing all around and serving up hot cocoa in big, ceramic mugs, and plates piled high with cookies, while a man came around and punched random letters into our tickets. That must've been a dream I'd had or a movie I watched one time.

Believe it or not, it was a long, dark ride through the snow covered wilderness. And the cocoa we drank was watery and served in a paper cup that my mother had put some cardboard rings around so it wouldn't burn our hands. And the cookies were wrapped in cellophane...and stale.

In fact, had I not had a grand notion of what this

journey was going to be, I may very well have lost all hope right then and there.

But I knew there had to be more. I knew that the North Pole would be the attraction I was hoping to see, even if the train ride had left me a little underwhelmed.

It was a busy place, and I could feel the cold air envelope me as soon as the train stopped and doors slid open.

"Are you ready?" my father asked, a tinge of excitement in his eyes.

"I think so," I said. Though, to be perfectly honest, I knew that I was getting ready to do something that I could never come back from. I was going to, hopefully, be meeting Santa Claus and telling him that he'd made a huge mistake. I was really just hoping that I could go back to thinking of Christmas in the same warm, fuzzy ways I always had. But these experiences have a way of changing things.

And I didn't want Christmas to change at all.

*a*s I stepped off the train, onto the platform below, ice crunched beneath my feet, and my teeth began to chatter from the cold.

It was much colder than it had been at home, and that was pretty darn cold.

My parents stepped out after me, and my father put his hand on my back and guided me along, out of the way of the other passengers, who were trying to get off the train, and in a much bigger hurry, it seemed, than we were.

"Where do we go?" I asked. "What do we do?"

"I'm not exactly sure," my father said. "Somehow, I was expecting something a little more..."

"Christmas," my mother chimed in.

"Yeah," my father said, a confused look on his face. "This just looks like a normal train station."

He stepped in front of my mother and I, and said, "All my life, I've been dying to see this place. I've dreamt about it since the time my mother read me my first Christmas story as a child. And now that I'm finally here, I thought I'd see elves sledding, and reindeer flying, and cookies and wreaths, and presents, and something….much more than this."

He turned slowly, and extended his hand toward what lay in front of us, as if he was revealing the disappointment to himself.

"Not exactly a sight to behold," he muttered.

"There's got to be more to it than this," I said.

"Nelly's probably right, hon. Just be patient. We'll find what you've been dreaming of." My mother took my father by the hand and started leading him in the direction of the doors to the waiting area.

The room was bustling with passengers talking to workers behind the ticket counters, or talking on their cell phones with people back home about how their travel had been to this point, and what they were hoping for with the rest of it. There were a few benches off to my left where some men in suits were reading magazines and looking at their watches every few moments.

My father's head whipped from side to side, looking for the direction we were supposed to head.

"There," my mother said, pointing over his shoulder, directing his gaze to a tiny door in the corner.

That definitely looked like the place.

The door was about half the size of a normal door. My father and mother would certainly have to duck to get through it. It looked to be made of wood and was painted a vibrant red. On the door, hanging about halfway down was a beautiful pine wreath with a decadent gold bow. In the center of the wreath, I could make out a big, brass knocker.

The sign above the door jutted out into the room, like a street sign, and read *North Pole*.

"That's funny," my father mused. "I thought we were at the North Pole already. Hmmm..." He raised his eyebrow and looked at me. I could see in his face that the excitement within him was rising again, as the realization that this waiting room we were in wasn't our final destination. The idea that we had more in store for us spurred him on! "It appears as though our journey is not yet over!"

He walked briskly across the waiting room, and my mother and I struggled to keep up.

When we got to the door, my father put his hand on the polished brass knob and turned.

"Locked," he said. His shoulders dropped and he let out the once excited air that he'd been holding in his lungs.

"It's okay," my mother said. "Maybe we just have to knock first." She pointed at the knocker in the center of the wreath.

He puffed out his chest a little bit.

"You, know, you might be right." He turned and looked at me. "What do you say, Nelly? Do you want to do the honors?"

"Yes!" I shouted. I stepped forward and put my hands on the cold brass and pulled it back. And then, with the excitement of a kid rushing down the stairs on Christmas morning, I thrust it forward.

With the noise that surrounded us, it was difficult to hear anything.

We stood there for a moment.

Nothing happened.

"Try it again," my mother said.

I nodded and brought my hand up to the knocker yet again. But before I was able to grip it, the door began to open.

10

*J*could feel something rising up into my throat, as the door slowly worked its way back. It swung slowly on its hinges. My stomach was like a roller coaster, flipping and flopping back and forth. I was just dying to find out what was on the other side.

When the door completed its journey, my parents and I stared into darkness.

There was no sign, that we could see, at least, of who or what had opened the door.

We didn't know if it had opened by itself, or if it had been pulled open by someone. And we had no idea if we were supposed to enter or not.

I looked up at my mother. She had a confused look on her face. She was wrinkling her eyebrows and pursing her lips, trying to figure out what we were to do next.

My eyes moved from my mother's pensive face to my father's. His face was less pensive, and more confused. He brought his right hand up and scratched the top of his head.

I wanted to ask them what we were supposed to do, but thought better of it. I knew those faces of theirs well, and they were already telling me, without any words at all, that they didn't have the slightest clue.

A few moments passed, and then a faint noise that hadn't been present before, entered the cacophony of the busy train station.

It was a small grunting.

And with every tiny grunt we heard, we could see the door jostling slightly back and forth.

When the door finished moving and came to rest again, the grunting subsided. In its place came the sound of heavy breathing.

I had gathered that someone had been behind the door, and had worked their way out and was now trying to catch their breath.

But who?

In the darkness, my parents and I were unable to make out who was there.

As the breathing slowed, we got our first glimpse of a foot.

It was wearing a pointy green shoe, that curled up at

the toe. The shoe was made of something that looked like very expensive felt.

A moment after that, another shoe emerged. This one was exactly the same as the first one, and took its place right next to it.

I brought my eyes up, and saw stockings that had a red and white candy cane design, leading up to puffy green knickers.

Above the knickers, was a tiny little pot belly that was covered in a green felt jacket that matched the shoes and knickers perfectly. Five shiny gold buttons drew my eyes up to the face, which was bare and smooth.

His chin was pointed, and his cheeks were flushed red. Beneath his jet black hair, he had the brightest blue eyes I'd ever seen. And his ears were pointed, and looked to be holding his bright green cap in place.

I thought I'd have been speechless if I were ever to meet a real life North Pole elf.

But I was the opposite. In fact, words just started popping out.

"Are you an elf? Do you know Santa? Is Rudolph real? Do you think I could meet him? I've always dreamed about coming here you know? I'm very excited! Christmas is my favorite holiday of all time — I just thought you should know that because, you know, I'm on the naughty list. But I don't really understand why. Do you think that I could talk to Santa about that? Because

I've really been a good girl this year. I'm not a bad person at all, and so this must all be some kind of mix up…"

I felt my father put his hands on my shoulders. I also felt his breath against my ears, though in my verbal assault of the small figure in front of me, I didn't exactly hear any of what he said.

But I got the gist anyway.

Finally, the elf spoke.

"Welcome to the North Pole," he said. "Please come in."

11

I had expected the elf to say more to us than he did.

Instead, he silently led us down a dark corridor full of right turns, followed by left turns, and then more rights. He was holding a lantern next to his side. It swung back and forth, and gave us no view of our surroundings, only of where he was.

I found myself thinking that if I had to get out of here on my own, there was no way I could ever do it. To say I was nervous was a bit of an understatement.

For one, I was on the naughty list, and had dared to make this journey in the first place. I mean, that act alone might be enough to wipe out a year of good behavior for most kids.

For two, this elf that was leading the way refused to speak to us past his opening sentence or two. What was his problem?

Perhaps, I'd scared him. I think that if I had it to do again, I might just start with saying something like, "Hi, I'm Penelope Ann Dingman, and I was hoping to see Santa."

I don't know.

Something like that, perhaps.

Something that was a little bit better at breaking the ice and helping him let his guard down.

But, I hadn't done that. I'd done what I did, and now we walked in silence, without so much as an assurance that everything was going to be okay.

My father and mother were nervous too. I could tell by the way they were holding my hand as we made our way through the darkness.

Mother's hand was gripping mine tightly. She kept gripping, and re-gripping as we walked, never satisfied or comfortable with the level of tightness of her hand on mine.

From where I was standing, it was definitely tight enough.

And my father's hand was so sweaty as we walked that he kept letting go and wiping his palm on his pants before finding me again. This happened several times, and each time he returned his hand to mine it was a little sweatier than the time before.

After what seemed like hours, we were starting to pick up a smell.

I could hear my father sniffing hard in the air. And then his hand started to pulsate its grip. He started to shake my hand up and down with his.

"Do you smell that?" he whispered.

"Mint?" I whispered back.

"Yes!" he said. "Peppermint, to be exact — just like a candy cane."

"We are getting close," the elf said. "Just a few more turns and we'll be there."

Another right, and a quick left and we were at another door.

The elf reached out his right hand, opened the door, and spun fluidly out with it. He bowed and extended his left hand in the direction of the smell.

It took a moment for my eyes to adjust to the flood of light that had come rushing into them.

"Do you see that, Nelly!" my father exulted. I felt his arms wrap around my shoulders and shake me excitedly.

I slowly started to peel my squinted eyes apart.

My mother let go of my hand and was gasping.

When I was finally able to open my eyes and behold what my parents had been speaking about, I realized that their reactions had not done this place justice.

It was better than I could have ever imagined it. And we were here.

We were standing right in the middle of The North Pole!

$\mathcal{W}$e were standing at the base of a giant tree. I looked behind us and the elf who'd led us through the corridor and out into this Christmas dream was speaking to another elf.

The new elf was nodding his head as the elf that had brought us this far was relaying his story. I could tell that he was impersonating me and trying as best he could to tell this new elf every detail of what I'd said.

After a moment, they shook hands and the elf that had brought us here, disappeared behind the door and closed it, making the trunk of this tree we were under whole again.

The elf that approached us now was dressed exactly the same as the elf that led us here. The only real difference between the two, was this elf had a long grey beard and a few wrinkles on his ruddy cheeks.

My father was looking up above us. There were branches and pine needles all adorned with different kinds of ornaments — bulbs, rocking horses, and, of course, candy canes...lots and lots of candy canes.

"This is awesome," he said, mostly to himself, though we were all able to hear him.

"Agreed," the oldish looking elf said, nodding. "It is quite awesome here!"

My father brought his attention down to the man standing in front of us.

He must not have been paying attention while the two elves were talking to each other. Rather, he was transfixed by the whole giant Christmas tree thing.

"You look different than you did before," he said to our new guide. He put his hand up to his mouth and said, "Oh, wow! Did you just grow that beard? How did you get all that hair to come out of your face so fast? It's magic, right? Christmas magic!" He snapped and wagged his finger at the elf. "You're good! This place is amazing!"

The elf looked at my mother and I with concern. It was clear that he was looking at us for some indication as to whether my father was crazy or not.

My mother shrugged her shoulders and said, "I think he was paying attention to something else while you and the other guy were talking."

The elf let out a large breath of air. "Whew, that's a relief." He then held out his hand and introduced himself to us. We each took turns shaking it as he said, "My name is Shinny. I'm the oldest elf around these parts." He brought his hands up to mouth and spoke behind it, "I'm even older than the big man himself!"

"Wow!" my father said, grabbing the frail looking elf's hand with both of his and shaking it vigorously up and down. "A real pleasure to meet you."

When my father finally let go, Shinny took a step backward and examined his hand, giving it a limp shake. "That's quite a grip you've got there, sonny."

"Sorry," my father replied. "I guess I let my excitement get the best of me."

"That's understandable. It actually happens quite a lot," Shinny nodded. "But these bone's aren't getting any younger, you know!"

We stood there for a second waiting for Shinny to finish feeling his hand and making sure that nothing was cracked or broken.

"Anyway," he finally said, "what brings you all the way up here?"

"Well," my mother stepped forward, putting her hand out to hold my father at bay. "Our daughter, Penelope, has received a rather disturbing letter. You see, she's been notified that she's on the 'Naughty' list."

"Imagine that," Shinny said, giving me a side eyed

glance. "Let me guess, you're here to talk to someone and have her put back on the 'Nice' list, is that it?"

"Yes," my mother smiled.

"No way," Shinny shook his head. "No can do. Nodda. Not gonna happen. No way no how."

"I'm sorry?" my mother said.

My father made a move forward, but again my mother held him back.

I did my best to fight the tears that were welling up. This had not been how I'd expected this to go. I had been certain that I would be granted a meeting with someone to plead my case, to be heard about this whole mix up. And now, this old elf, with far too much hair shooting out his ears was standing between me and my rightful place on the 'Nice' list, telling us there was nothing that could be done.

It was more than I could bear.

I started to sob, big heaving cries into the pine and peppermint scented air.

Shinny turned and looked at me. "That must be Penelope," he said.

"It is," my mother told him. "And she's quite devastated by this whole thing. You see, she's really a nice girl. Not perfect, mind you. But nice. Sure she doesn't pick up her room all the time, and she doesn't always do her homework when I ask her, but she does enough right to be on the proper list."

Shinny stood up straight, leaning back slightly, rubbing his chin with his right hand, using his left arm as a perch.

"Is this true, Penelope?" he asked. "Are you a generally good person?"

I nodded, as the tears began to roll off my cheeks and onto my coat.

"I don't usually do this," Shinny took a deep breath. "But with most of the parents that come here with their kids, claiming that they've been put on the wrong list, it's quite easy to tell that the right decision has been made. Their kids are usually trying to climb up this tree and grab free candy canes, or they bolt into Christmas village looking to get their grubby little mitts on any little piece of 'the season' that they can. But you're different. I can sense that."

I wiped the tears from my eyes and stood up a little taller.

My father stopped his charge and asked, "So, you're going to let us see Santa?"

"Santa?" Shinny laughed. "Oh, heavens no. I'm sorry folks, but this close to Christmas, nobody gets access to Santa...least of all, people who climb aboard a train and come up here on a whim without so much as making a proper appointment."

"I'm confused," my father said. "It just sounded like

you were going to hear our case. It sounded like you were telling us that you'd give us a chance."

"Oh, I'm going to. But this problem doesn't require Santa's involvement. This problem is a simple system override. And for that, we must go through the proper channels."

"There are 'proper channels' at the North Pole?" my mother asked.

"Yes. Yes, there are," Shinny said. "Imagine this. If your daughter came home with a failing grade on a test, you wouldn't contact the Superintendent of the school district, would you?"

"No," my mother laughed. "That's just silly. We'd talk to her teacher."

"Correct," Shinny said, putting a stiff finger in the air. "Well, it's clear to me that we have a list issue. And we have an elf here who's in charge of all the list issues."

"So, you're going to let us see him?" my father asked.

"Yes," Shinny said, turning on his heels and walking away from us, toward the edge of the tree branches. "Follow me."

13

"*H*is name is Alabaster," Shinny said as he led us through the wonder that was the North Pole.

The buildings all around us were small and quaint, each with their own little chimneys, which were puffing perfect clouds of smoke out into the air.

Smells of cookies and pies of all kinds could be smelled as I walked briskly to keep up with Shinny and hear what he said. It was almost too much for me to take in and still stay focused.

But somehow, I'd managed. I was on the Naughty list, after all. And staying focused on the task at hand was the only way I was ever going to get off of it.

"Alabaster's in charge of all things list related. He has over a hundred elves that he employs to help him keep things straight. It's a mighty task." Shinny turned and looked at us, his eyes soft. He shrugged as he said, "Sometimes, mistakes get made." And then his eyes hardened again, and he looked directly at me. "Then again, sometimes they don't."

I felt uncomfortable being judged by Shinny. But, then again, what had I expected? I'm sure they get hundreds of kids a year, if not more, claiming that they've been wrongly accused of being naughty.

I was just one more.

"Oh, well," Shinny said, throwing his hands up in the air and turning back to his path, "I guess we'll find out soon enough!"

We followed him for a few more minutes as we passed the sleigh repair shop, where it looked like there were at least ten sleighs waiting to be worked on. We also passed the reindeer stables, where all of Santa's flying friends were taken care of. Trust me when I tell you, it didn't smell magical at all. It smelled like dried up hay and animal droppings. In the door frame, someone had hung some oranges that had been used as a sort of pin cushion for cloves.

Unfortunately, this didn't make the smell of the barn any less pungent. Rather, it added a sickly sweet and spicy scent that made the feeling that I might vomit just that much stronger.

I was thankful to be past that place and on our way.

The last thing we passed before getting to our destination was a house that looked rather unremarkable. It was a tiny little thing, built of stone, with a few tiny windows and a green, wooden door in the front.

"That's where Santa's bags are made," Shinny smiled and pointed. "You know, the ones he uses to carry all of the toys. Strongest bags in the world, those are!"

As we approached Alabaster's offices, which was a very large building that looked like a giant post office or law firm, Shinny took one second to look off into the distance.

He pointed toward a large house up on a snow covered hill. There was a long path leading up toward it, and smoke could be seen rising up through the chimney and into the crisp northern air. The windows were fogged with condensation.

"Do you see that place, there?" Shinny asked us.

"Yes," my mother answered.

"That's his house." A smile broke across Shinny's face. "Beautiful, isn't it?"

We nodded our agreement.

Shinny stood there for a moment longer, clearly reliving fond memories from all of his years serving Santa at the North Pole.

"Good man, that Santa," he said as he composed himself and prepared to open the door. On the door, were two words: THE LIST. "This is our final stop today.

Follow me closely when we get inside. It's a bit busy, especially this time of year, what with it being so close to the big day."

He gave us a nod and a wink and then opened the door.

We stepped inside, and I was not prepared for what we encountered next.

14

*E*ven with Shinny's warning, the number and speed at which the elves inside moved through the halls, going about their daily business, seemed overwhelming.

I was grabbing onto my father's coat as he moved forward. My mother grabbed onto me. And my father was trying to grab onto Shinny.

But he was moving faster than we could, as he was quite a bit smaller than we were.

And as we got farther into the hallway, it became harder to locate which one of these elves was Shinny.

From our vantage point, they all started to look the same with their green hats and diminutive stature.

"I lost him," my father's panicked voice called.

"Me too," my mother said.

I squinted and tried to find him in the crowd. It took a moment or two, and I still have no idea how I was able to do it, but I found him.

He was about ten feet in front of us, turning right down a narrow hallway.

"There!" I yelled and pointed at him.

"Let's go!" my father exclaimed.

The next thing I knew, my mother and I were being dragged by my father through the lobby of THE LIST building and toward the hallway Shinny'd just turned down.

I found myself bumping into quite a few elves along the way. They were bouncing off my mother and father's legs, but I was quite a bit shorter than they were, so I got to see them up close and personal.

And they weren't happy about being shoved out of their way. Their eyes met mine, and the looks behind their black pupils and stony blue irises were enough to make me feel like, perhaps, I really did belong on the naughty list.

"Hey! Watch it!" some said.

"What's the big idea," another called out.

"Sorry," I said, as my father pulled me through wave after wave of angry men in green felt suits.

"You've gotta lotta nerve, man," one elf called out to my father. My father, in his haste, ignored everything.

The whole ordeal only lasted ten or twenty seconds,

and was punctuated with an exclamation point by a particularly youngish looking elf, who stopped right in his tracks and bellowed, "DUDE!!!"

As we rounded the corner to the hallway we'd seen Shinny walk down, we quickly realized that all of what we'd just done was completely unnecessary.

Shinny was standing in the hallway with his hands raised and shoulders shrugged, as if to ask, "What was that all about?"

He was alone.

The hallway was completely empty except for us...and Shinny.

He was standing in front of an elevator.

"I was waiting for you, you know..." Shinny said.

My father just nodded as his neck and face turned red. "At least, I'll have a cool story to tell my friends when I get home."

Shinny rolled his eyes and the elevator doors opened.

"Get in folks," he said. "We're almost there."

15

I knew the elevator was moving up through the floors of the building quickly. All of the indicators were there. My stomach was flopping, I felt slightly off balance, and the lights on the control panel were changing every second to indicate a new floor had been reached.

That didn't stop it from feeling like it was taking forever. I wanted to get to wherever we were headed so fast. I wanted to stand in front of Alabaster and plead my case and tell him that he and all of his elves had made a mistake and put an innocent girl on the wrong list.

As we moved closer to the top floor, where Shinny'd told us Alabaster's office was, my mouth went dry.

Nerves.

I had to find some way to calm myself down or I

wouldn't be able to tell him what I needed to tell him in the way that I needed to be able to tell him.

My palms were sweating, and my stomach now had to deal with the flip floppy feeling of the elevator plus the butterflies that had just started to flutter around.

I wiped my palms on the outside of my coat and put my hands together. Then I closed my eyes and took long, deep breaths. In through my nose and out through my mouth.

"What's that all about?" Shinny asked my parents. "Is she okay?"

"She's fine," my mother stepped in and answered. "She's just doing some deep breathing, trying to focus her mind on the task in front of her."

"That's very interesting," Shinny nodded. "I've never seen anything like that. Usually, the kids who end up coming this far start getting tired of trying to act good and throw a huge tantrum. In fact," Shinny put a finger into the air, "I can only remember three kids actually holding it together long enough to speak with Alabaster about his list."

"Only three?" my father inquired.

"Yup."

"And how did those times go? Were they able to get off the naughty list?"

"Oh," Shinny said, "no, not even close. When Alabaster started to reference the video footage, their cases fell apart completely. And then the tantrums came, and they had to be dragged back onto the elevator kicking and screaming — which is kind of embarrassing, you know. I mean, this is a place of business." He stood up tall and gave a prideful little tug on his felt jacket. "Know what I mean?"

"I think so," my father replied, though the look on his face said otherwise.

There was a sudden jolt below our feet, and my stomach flopped for the last time. The flutters were still strong, and my palms were still sweaty, and my mouth was dryer than flour caked hands, but all of the uncomfortable elevator symptoms had subsided now that we'd reached our destination.

Before we stepped out into yet another hallway, I looked up toward the sky and called in a prayer favor. I had a feeling that if Santa and Alabaster weren't quite on my side yet, that maybe a little extra help from the original Big Man might be needed.

A quick 'Amen' and I was stepping off the elevator, and staring down a narrow corridor with a big brown door at the opposite end, and nothing more.

We walked the length of the corridor. It was the longest twenty seven feet of my life, and yes, I was counting my steps.

On the door was a sign that read:

The Office of
Alabaster Snowball
Overseer of THE LIST
Serious Inquiries Only

I took one last, deep breath as Shinny knocked on the door, and prepared myself for the meeting that would change my life forever.

16

*T*he first thing I noticed was that the room was stuffy. There was a tiny window, on a wall to my right, that allowed a sliver of light to come in and illuminate a small portion of the space.

I could see the individual dust particles floating into the slice of yellow, as they fell like snow onto the objects below.

There were books everywhere, and old rolls of parchment that had been rolled up tightly and sealed with red wax. They were neatly organized on the ceiling to floor bookshelves that lined both sides of the room.

I'd have liked to have had the time to study my surroundings a little further, but there was an elf waiting for us at his desk.

He was short, and wore green felt like the others we'd

seen thus far. His face was gaunt and full of wrinkles, and the hair that slipped out from beneath his hat was white as the snow that fell from the sky.

In front of the desk there were three chairs, set up all in a row, as though they'd been expecting us.

Shinny led us to the chairs and put a hand out, inviting us to take our seats.

I took the seat in the middle, my mother to my left and my father to my right.

Shinny then introduced us.

"Penelope, Mr. and Mrs. Dingman, this is is Alabaster Snowball. He is the overseer of Santa's list."

"Pleased to me meet you," my father said, reaching a hand forward.

Alabaster leaned forward and shook it.

My mother was more reserved and gave a quiet wave and a nod and said, "Nice to meet you."

I sat silently.

"A pleasure to meet you as well," Alabaster smiled as he released my father's hand and settled back into his seat.

Shinny looked at Alabaster and said, "If you don't mind, I'll be taking my leave now."

He bowed and Alabaster said, "I don't mind at all."

Shinny took a second to look at us and said, "It was very nice to meet you all. Good luck with everything. And Merry Christmas."

"Merry Christmas," we said, though at this moment in time, it was difficult for me to think of Christmas being merry this year.

As Shinny left, I felt my heart start to beat rapidly in my chest.

This was the moment I'd been waiting for, and we were finally here...and now, I didn't really want to know what Alabaster was going to say.

I didn't know if it would have been better without my parents, or not. Would it have been easier to sit in this chair without them?

The journey, to this point, had been much easier knowing that they were part of it, and knowing that if I needed anything, they'd have been there to lean on.

But now...now that we were in front of the one elf on the planet that knew about all of my nice moments, and all of my naughty moments, it suddenly wasn't so comforting to have my parents by my side.

I didn't really think I had anything to hide — but if I did, this Alabaster fellow would certainly trot it out and display it front and center.

My thoughts of woe were interrupted by Alabaster.

He'd put his hands in front of his face, covering his mouth with a deep, pensive triangle of fingers.

"This isn't easy for my to say," he said, looking deep into my eyes with his marble blue stare.

I swallowed hard. Here it came. He was going to tell

my parents and I that I belonged on the 'Naughty List' and that I'd earned my rightful spot on it. And that there was nothing I could do except go home and clean up my act so that I didn't end up on it again next year.

My mind raced as I thought about all of the horrible things that would happen if I were to make the list two years in a row. Are kids who are on the list for two consecutive years even allowed to celebrate Christmas after that?

All of these thoughts were swept away, however, when Alabaster continued.

"We've made a mistake."

17

I looked up at my parents, wondering what their reaction was going to be. My father looked at my mother and shrugged. My mother looked at my father and shrugged. And then they both looked at me and shrugged.

We turned our gazes back to the elf across the wide mahogany desk.

"What does that mean?" my father asked.

Alabaster took a deep breath in and then exhaled slowly.

"I'm sorry to say that my department made a mistake. An error. To put it bluntly, we screwed up."

"I don't understand," my mother said, a slight twinge of relief in her voice.

"It happens from time to time. It seems that on this

particular occasion, an elf named Tiny made the error. She's normally very good about things, but this time... not so much," Alabaster said, separating his hands as he explained. "You see, we have so many children to take note of, that on occasion one of them will end up on the wrong list. Fortunately, it usually ends up with a kid who should be on the 'Naughty List' accidentally being put on the 'Nice List'.

"It's much better to give people the benefit of the doubt, rather than take things away when we're not one hundred percent sure.

"But sometimes it works the other way, too. Thankfully, it's only happened three times under my watch. And that's saying something," he said, puffing out his chest. "I've been at the helm here for over five hundred years. Unfortunately, Penelope, you were my third mistake."

I swallowed hard. What did this mean? Obviously, I'd done nothing wrong, and he was apologizing for that. But, what did it mean for me and this Christmas in a few days? Was it too late to put me on the right list?

I had so many emotions swirling around in my mind that I just blurted it out.

"So, am I going to get coal this year?"

It felt wrong, and a little ungrateful to just come out with it like that, but I'd had so many emotions running through my mind, and I'd held everything in for so long that it just sort of popped out.

"Oh, heavens no," Alabaster smiled. "My dear, here at the North Pole we believe in making things right. In fact, as a result of our little mix up, you're going to have one the best Christmas you've ever had. Plus," he stuck a finger in the air, "we've got a special surprise for you before you go back home today!"

"What's that?" my mother asked.

"Well," Alabaster said, standing up and walking to a door on the back wall of his office, "why don't I show you."

18

*W*e stood up and followed Alabaster through the door. My legs were like jelly, and I hadn't quite digested all of the news about the list mix up and what that meant for me.

Even though I knew it was all going to be good, there was a part of me that was still reeling at the whole experience.

That thought was shoved aside rather quickly, however, when I saw what was on the other side of the door.

The smell of sugar cookies and minty gum drops hit my nose at the same time as a heavy set man with a fluffy, white beard came into my view.

He was wearing bright red, crushed velvet pants that were being held up by suspenders over a long sleeved red shirt. His boots were big and black, just like I'd seen in pictures.

"Santa!" my father exclaimed. He rushed the man like a child and hugged him around his mid-section.

I'd never seen my father put his whole head underneath another man's armpit before, but I guess seeing Santa makes even the most grown up of adults act like children.

"Ho, ho, ho, there mister," Santa chuckled as he put his hands on my father's shoulder and tried to keep the two of them from toppling into Mrs. Claus, who was walking by with a tray of cookies and milk.

"Nice save, Santa," she said as she put the tray down on a small, round table in the middle of the room. "I've made some cookies and milk for you folks. You know, for all the trouble you've been through."

"That's very kind of you," my mother said. "But it hasn't been that much trouble. It's actually been pretty neat to see how things work up here!"

Mrs. Claus nodded and said, "Well, please enjoy a cookie anyway. We're very fond of cookies up here, you know." She gave me a little wink that made me feel all warm and fuzzy inside.

I walked over and took a cookie off the tray and had a bite. It was bliss...no, it was better. It was like Heaven in my mouth. Never before in my life, and never again, would I ever taste a cookie like that one that Mrs. Claus made. It was sugary and soft and warm and buttery. So good.

While I was enjoying my cookie, Santa was able to free himself from my father's grasp. He made his way over to me.

"Penelope," he said, looking down at me. "I'm terribly sorry about the mix up. We pride ourselves on not letting that happen, but every now and then we have a night where nothing goes right. I'm afraid that happened a few days ago, and as a result, you received a letter that should never have been sent."

He shrugged, and after a moment asked, "Can you find it in your heart to forgive us?"

Wait!

Had I heard that correctly?

Not only was I eating the best cookie I'd ever tasted, prepared by Mrs. Claus, herself, but Santa was asking for my forgiveness.

I pinched my arm, checking to make sure that this wasn't some kind of wonderful dream.

I nodded, "Yes, Santa, I forgive you."

The words felt strange as they came out, like I was watching myself speak them from a distance.

"Thank you," Santa said. "I have to get going now, but I do have something else for you, Penelope."

I wanted to tell him to call me Nelly, but I was in such

awe that I just waited there for him to reveal what he had.

He reached into his pants pocket and pulled out an envelope.

"These are special tickets," he said. "They will allow you and your family to make an appointment with me any time from New Year's Day until Thanksgiving. That way we can spend some real time together, and I can give you the full tour of the North Pole personally. Oh, and we'll also have a fantastic feast prepared by Mrs. Claus." He winked and said, "If you think those cookies are good, just you wait and see what else she can make."

I could feel the smile form on my face as I took the envelope from him.

He put his finger in the air. "Hold on just a minute. There's one more thing...I almost forgot."

Reaching into his other pocket, he pulled out another envelope. This one was red.

"These are train tickets back to your house. Please do not take the normal train you took to get up here. This is a special train reserved for very good boys and girls. I think you'll find this one more to your liking."

He smiled as he handed me the envelope. I felt my father put his hand on my shoulder.

I looked up at him and saw that there were tears running down his cheeks. Apparently the joy of meeting his childhood hero was too much for him to keep bottled up.

Santa took a moment and checked his watch. "Oh dear, I've got to go. Terribly sorry. I look forward to seeing you next year."

He turned to leave. My father called out, "Santa?"

Santa turned back.

"Could you say, 'Ho, ho, ho', one more time?"

Santa rolled his eyes and shook his head.

"Ho, ho, ho," he bellowed. "Now, if you'll excuse me, I really do have to go."

He gave a wave and turned with a jerk, and was on his way to bigger things.

And my father was a wet, snotty heap, crying tears of joy and eating sugar cookies made by Mrs. Claus, soaking in the final few minutes of his dream trip.

19

*T*he train ride back didn't disappoint. The seats were bright red leather and the floor was covered in a vibrant green carpet.

We sat in a booth with another family that had bags of stuff that they'd purchased from their trip to the North Pole. These were souvenirs like elf hats and Santa beards and things like that.

They were all wearing their pajamas as we prepared to depart.

There was a large table between us, in the middle of the seats.

Before the train left the station, the table had been filled with cookies of all kinds, and candies, and giant carafes of hot chocolate.

The man who brought them to the table came back

with some tall mugs and said, "Everything you see is one hundred percent complimentary. Please, have as much as you'd like...or as much as your parents will allow." He winked at the man across from my father.

We all chuckled at that, except for the little boy in the seat across from us. He looked downright disappointed by the remark, but to be fair, he only looked to be about five or six years old.

The train lurched forward after a few minutes and we started to move at a steady pace. The man who'd delivered our food worked his way past all of the other tables that were filled with excited kids and tired looking parents.

He grabbed a microphone off the wall at the front of the car and said, "Welcome, ladies and gentlemen. Thank you for joining us at the North Pole today. We hope you enjoyed your visit. Our destination today is home."

My father and mother looked at each other and shrugged, as though they found something strange.

The man continued. "As we travel, you'll hear an assortment of Classic Christmas songs. Please feel free to join in and sing when the spirit moves you. That is all for now. Enjoy the ride and we'll see you at home!"

He put the microphone down and 'Jingle Bells' started playing.

We listened to the Christmas songs and sang and ate for the better part of an hour, and then all of the sudden, the people on the train started to disappear, family by family.

They were gone.

And a moment later, the train was gone, and my father and mother and I were standing in front of our snow covered front walk on Lincoln Street, staring up at our dark and quiet house.

The Christmas tree lights were on in the window.

I took a deep breath of cold, crisp winter air, took my parents by the hands and said, "Thank you."

And then, together, we walked toward our home, ready for a restful night, full of happy dreams as we prepared for the best Christmas yet.

YOU MIGHT ALSO ENJOY!

*I*f you enjoyed this story, you might also enjoy these!

When Evan tries to travel to Pluto and crash lands on the North Pole, he gets the experience dreams are made of! Join him as he learns all about he inner workings of Santa's Workshop! Click on the book cover to read this wonderful story that will get the whole family in the mood for the Christmas season!

When JW finds out he has super powers, he has to decide how he's going to use them. And he soon discovers, being a super hero isn't all it's cracked up to be! Click on the cover to read this exciting trilogy of superhero stories!

When Zack Benefeld's life is tipped upside down when an alien crash lands in his room, he has more than a few problems to deal with! Click on the book cover to read this fun story about a boy and his alien!

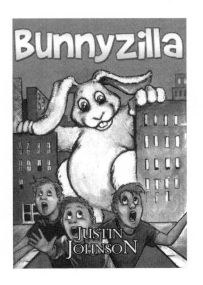

Ricky Jenkins wanted a bunny for Easter. Mr. Whiskers was the runt of the litter. Now, Mr. Whiskers is over 200 feet tall and terrorizing the city! Click on the book cover to read this fast paced thrill ride!

Someone Made a Big Mistake!

An eclectic group of elves, in charge of helping with the Naughty List, accidentally make the mother of all mistakes. This night will surely go down as The Night Nothing Went Right!
Available for the Christmas Season
November 2018!

December's finally here
That could only mean one thing...

The Great Tree Lighting

KIDS

JUSTIN JOHNSON

Coming for Christmas 2018!

$\mathcal{I}$ write...a lot! If you'd like to look through any of my books, feel free to click on the link above or search me on Amazon to check out my Amazon Author Page. Here, you'll find all of my books in all of their formats (ebook, paperback, and audio!).

Thank you for reading my stories!

Justin Johnson

Made in the USA
Monee, IL
17 November 2022